The Tale of the Bamboo Cutter (竹取物語 Taketori Monogatari) is a 10th-century Japanese monogatari (fictional prose narrative) containing folkloric elements. It is considered the oldest extant Japanese prose narrative although the oldest manuscript dates to 1592.

It was also occasionally known as The Tale of Princess Kaguya (かぐや姫の物語 Kaguya-hime no Monogatari), after its protagonist. It primarily details the life of a mysterious girl called Kaguya-hime, who was discovered as a baby inside the stalk of a glowing bamboo plan

Long, long ago, there lived an old bamboo wood-cutter. He was very poor and sad also, for no child had Heaven sent to cheer his old age, and in his heart there was no hope of rest from work till he died and was laid in the quiet grave. Every morning he went forth into the woods and hills wherever the bamboo reared its lithe green plumes against the sky. When he had made his choice, he would cut down these feathers of the forest, and splitting them lengthwise, or cutting them into joints, would carry the bamboo wood home and make it into various articles for the household, and he and his old wife gained a small livelihood by selling them.

One morning as usual he had gone out to his work, and having found a nice clump of bamboos, had set to work to cut some of them down. Suddenly the green grove of bamboos was flooded with a bright soft light, as if the full moon had risen over the spot. Looking round in astonishment, he saw that the brilliance was streaming from one bamboo. The old man, full of wonder, dropped his ax and went towards the light. On nearer approach he saw that this soft splendor came from a hollow in the green bamboo stem, and still more wonderful to behold, in the midst of the brilliance stood a tiny human being, only three inches in height, and exquisitely beautiful in appearance.

"You must be sent to be my child, for I find you here among the bamboos where lies my daily work," said the old man, and taking the little creature in his hand he took it home to his wife to bring up. The tiny girl was so exceedingly beautiful and so small, that the old woman put her into a basket to safeguard her from the least possibility of being hurt in any way.

The old couple were now very happy, for it had been a lifelong regret that they had no children of their own, and with joy they now expended all the love of their old age on the little child who had come to them in so marvelous a manner.

From this time on, the old man often found gold in the notches of the bamboos when he hewed them down and cut them up; not only gold, but precious stones also, so that by degrees he became rich. He built himself a fine house, and was no longer known as the poor bamboo woodcutter, but as a wealthy man.

Three months passed quickly away, and in that time the bamboo child had, wonderful to say, become a full-grown girl, so her foster-parents did up her hair and dressed her in beautiful kimonos. She was of such wondrous beauty that they placed her behind the screens like a princess, and allowed no one to see her, waiting upon her themselves. It seemed as if she were made of light, for the house was filled with a soft shining, so that even in the dark of night it was like daytime. Her presence seemed to have a benign influence on those there. Whenever the old man felt sad, he had only to look upon his foster-daughter and his sorrow vanished, and he became as happy as when he was a youth.

At last the day came for the naming of their new-found child, so theold couple called in a celebrated name-giver, and he gave her the nameof Princess Moonlight, because her body gave forth so much soft bright light that she might have been a daughter of the Moon God.

For three days the festival was kept up with song and dance and music. All the friends and relations of the old couple were present, and great was their enjoyment of the festivities held to celebrate the naming of Princess Moonlight. Everyone who saw her declared that there never had been seen any one so lovely; all the beauties throughout the length and breadth of the land would grow pale beside her, so they said. The fame of the Princess's loveliness spread far and wide, and many were the suitors who desired to win her hand, or even so much as to see her.

Suitors from far and near posted themselves outside the house, and made little holes in the fence, in the hope of catching a glimpse of the Princess as she went from one room to the other along the veranda. They stayed there day and night, sacrificing even their sleep for a chance of seeing her, but all in vain. Then they approached the house, and tried to speak to the old man and his wife or some of the servants, but not even this was granted them.

Still, in spite of all this disappointment they stayed on day after day, and night after night, and counted it as nothing, so great was their desire to see the Princess. At last, however, most of the men, seeing how hopeless their quest was, lost heart and hope both, and returned to their homes. All except five Knights, whose ardor and determination, instead of waning, seemed to wax greater with obstacles. These five men even went without their meals, and took snatches of whatever they could get brought to them, so that they might always stand outside the dwelling. They stood there in all weathers, in sunshine and in rain.

Sometimes they wrote letters to the Princess, but no answer was vouchsafed to them. Then when letters failed to draw any reply, they wrote poems to her telling her of the hopeless love which kept them from sleep, from food, from rest, and even from their homes. Still Princes Moonlight gave no sign of having received their verses.

In this hopeless state the winter passed. The snow and frost and the cold winds gradually gave place to the gentle warmth of spring. Then the summer came, and the sun burned white and scorching in the heavens above and on the earth beneath, and still these faithful Knights kept watch and waited. At the end of these long months they called out to the old bamboo-cutter and entreated him to have some mercy upon them and to show them the Princess, but he answered only that as he was not her real father he could not insist on her obeying him against her wishes.

The five Knights on receiving this stern answer returned to their several homes, and pondered over the best means of touching the proud Princess's heart, even so much as to grant them a hearing. They took their rosaries in hand and knelt before their household shrines, and burned precious incense, praying to Buddha to give them their heart's desire. Thus several days passed, but even so they could not rest in their homes.

So again they set out for the bamboo-cutter's house. This time the old man came out to see them, and they asked him to let them know if it was the Princess's resolution never to see any man whatsoever, and they implored him to speak for them and to tell her the greatness of their love, and how long they had waited through the cold of winter and the heat of summer, sleepless and roofless through all weathers, without food and without rest, in the ardent hope of winning her, and they were willing to consider this long vigil as pleasure if she would but give them one chance of pleading their cause with her. The old man lent a willing ear to their tale of love, for in his inmost heart he felt sorry for these faithful suitors and would have liked to see his lovely foster-daughter married to one of them. So he went in to Princess Moonlight and said reverently:

"Although you have always seemed to me to be a heavenly being, yet I have had the trouble of bringing you up as my own child and you have been glad of the protection of my roof. Will you refuse to do as I wish?"

Then Princess Moonlight replied that there was nothing she would not do for him, that she honored and loved him as her own father, and that as for herself she could not remember the time before she came to earth.

The old man listened with great joy as she spoke these dutiful words.

Then he told her how anxious he was to see her safely and happily married before he died.

"I am an old man, over seventy years of age, and my end may come any time now. It is necessary and right that you should see these five suitors and choose one of them."

"Oh, why," said the Princess in distress, "must I do this? I have no wish to marry now."

"I found you," answered the old man, "many years ago, when you were a little creature three inches high, in the midst of a great white light. The light streamed from the bamboo in which you were hid and led me to you. So I have always thought that you were more than mortal woman. While I am alive it is right for you to remain as you are if you wish to do so, but some day I shall cease to be and who will take care of you then? Therefore I pray you to meet these five brave men one at a time and make up your mind to marry one of them!"

Then the Princess answered that she felt sure that she was not as beautiful as perhaps report made her out to be, and that even if she consented to marry any one of them, not really knowing her before, his heart might change afterwards. So as she did not feel sure of them, even though her father told her they were worthy Knights, she did not feel it wise to see them.

"All you say is very reasonable," said the old man, "but what kind of men will you consent to see? I do not call these five men who have waited on you for months, light-hearted. They have stood outside this house through the winter and the summer, often denying themselves food and sleep so that they may win you. What more can you demand?"

Then Princess Moonlight said she must make further trial of their love before she would grant their request to interview her. The five warriors were to prove their love by each bringing her from distant countries something that she desired to possess.

That same evening the suitors arrived and began to play their flutes in turn, and to sing their self-composed songs telling of their great and tireless love. The bamboo-cutter went out to them and offered them his sympathy for all they had endured and all the patience they had shown in their desire to win his foster-daughter. Then he gave them her message, that she would consent to marry whosoever was successful in bringing her what she wanted. This was to test them.

The five all accepted the trial, and thought it an excellent plan, for it would prevent jealousy between them.

Princess Moonlight then sent word to the First Knight that she requested him to bring her the stone bowl which had belonged to Buddha in India.

The Second Knight was asked to go to the Mountain of Horai, said to be situated in the Eastern Sea, and to bring her a branch of the wonderful tree that grew on its summit. The roots of this tree were of silver, the trunk of gold, and the branches bore as fruit white jewels.

The Third Knight was told to go to China and search for the fire-rat and to bring her its skin. The Fourth Knight was told to search for the dragon that carried on its head the stone radiating five colors and to bring the stone to her.

The Fifth Knight was to find the swallow which carried a shell in its stomach and to bring the shell to her.

The old man thought these very hard tasks and hesitated to carry the messages, but the Princess would make no other conditions. So her commands were issued word for word to the five men who, when they heard what was required of them, were all disheartened and disgusted at what seemed to them the impossibility of the tasks given them and returned to their own homes in despair.

But after a time, when they thought of the Princess, the love in their hearts revived for her, and they resolved to make an attempt to get what she desired of them.

The First Knight sent word to the Princess that he was starting out that day on the quest of Buddha's bowl, and he hoped soon to bring it to her. But he had not the courage to go all the way to India, for in those days traveling was very difficult and full of danger, so he went to one of the temples in Kyoto and took a stone bowl from the altar there, paying the priest a large sum of money for it. He then wrapped it in a cloth of gold and, waiting quietly for three years, returned and carried it to the old man.

Princess Moonlight wondered that the Knight should have returned so soon. She took the bowl from its gold wrapping, expecting it to make the room full of light, but it did not shine at all, so she knew that it was a sham thing and not the true bowl of Buddha. She returned it at once and refused to see him. The Knight threw the bowl away and returned to his home in despair. He gave up now all hopes of ever winning the Princess.

The Second Knight told his parents that he needed change of air for his health, for he was ashamed to tell them that love for the Princess Moonlight was the real cause of his leaving them. He then left his home, at the same time sending word to the Princess that he was setting out for Mount Horai in the hope of getting her a branch of the gold and silver tree which she so much wished to have. He only allowed his servants to accompany him half-way, and then sent them back. He reached the seashore and embarked on a small ship, and after sailing away for three days he landed and employed several carpenters to build him a house contrived in such a way that no one could get access to it. He then shut himself up with six skilled jewelers, and endeavored to make such a gold and silver branch as he thought would satisfy the Princess as having come from the wonderful tree growing on Mount Horai. Every one whom he had asked declared that Mount Horai belonged to the land of fable and not to fact.

When the branch was finished, he took his journey home and tried to make himself look as if he were wearied and worn out with travel. He put the jeweled branch into a lacquer box and carried it to the bamboo-cutter, begging him to present it to the Princess.

The old man was quite deceived by the travel-stained appearance of the Knight, and thought that he had only just returned from his long journey with the branch. So he tried to persuade the Princess to consent to see the man. But she remained silent and looked very sad. The old man began to take out the branch and praised it as a wonderful treasure to be found nowhere in the whole land. Then he spoke of the Knight, how handsome and how brave he was to have undertaken a journey to so remote a place as the Mount of Horai.

Princess Moonlight took the branch in her hand and looked at it carefully. She then told her foster-parent that she knew it was impossible for the man to have obtained a branch from the gold and silver tree growing on Mount Horai so quickly or so easily, and she was sorry to say she believed it artificial.

The old man then went out to the expectant Knight, who had now approached the house, and asked where he had found the branch. Then the man did not scruple to make up a long story. "Two years ago I took a ship and started in search of Mount Horai. After going before the wind for some time I reached the far Eastern Sea. Then a great storm arose and I was tossed about for many days, losing all count of the points of the compass, and finally we were blown ashore on an unknown island. Here I found the place inhabited by demons who at one time threatened to kill and eat me. However, I managed to make friends with these horrible creatures, and they helped me and my sailors to repair the boat, and I set sail again. Our food gave out, and we suffered much from sickness on board. At last, on the five-hundredth day from the day of starting, I saw far off on the horizon what looked like the peak of a mountain. On nearer approach, this proved to be an island, in the center of which rose a high mountain. I landed, and after wandering about for two or three days, I saw a shining being coming towards me on the beach, holding in his hands a golden bowl. I went up to him and asked him if I had, by good chance, found the island of Mount Horai, and he answered:"

"'Yes, this is Mount Horai!'"

"With much difficulty I climbed to the summit, here stood the golden tree growing with silver roots in the ground. The wonders of that strange land are many, and if I began to tell you about them I could never stop. In spite of my wish to stay there long, on breaking off the branch I hurried back. With utmost speed it has taken me four hundred days to get back, and, as you see, my clothes are still damp from exposure on the long sea voyage. I have not even waited to change my raiment, so anxious was I to bring the branch to the Princess quickly."

Just at this moment the six jewelers, who had been employed on the making of the branch, but not yet paid by the Knight, arrived at the house and sent in a petition to the Princess to be paid for their labor. They said that they had worked for over a thousand days making the branch of gold, with its silver twigs and its jeweled fruit, that was now presented to her by the Knight, but as yet they had received nothing in payment. So this Knight's deception was thus found out, and the Princess, glad of an escape from one more importunate suitor, was only too pleased to send back the branch. She called in the workmen and had them paid liberally, and they went away happy. But on the way home they were overtaken by the disappointed man, who beat them till they were nearly dead, for letting out the secret, and they barely escaped with their lives. The Knight then returned home, raging in his heart; and in despair of ever winning the Princess gave up society and retired to a solitary life among the mountains.

Now the Third Knight had a friend in China, so he wrote to him to get the skin of the fire-rat. The virtue of any part of this animal was that no fire could harm it. He promised his friend any amount of money he liked to ask if only he could get him the desired article. As soon as the news came that the ship on which his friend had sailed home had come into port, he rode seven days on horseback to meet him. He handed his friend a large sum of money, and received the fire-rat's skin. When he reached home he put it carefully in a box and sent it in to the Princess while he waited outside for her answer.

The bamboo-cutter took the box from the Knight and, as usual, carried it in to her and tried to coax her to see the Knight at once, but Princess Moonlight refused, saying that she must first put the skin to test by putting it into the fire. If it were the real thing it would not burn.

So she took off the crape wrapper and opened the box, and then threw the skin into the fire. The skin crackled and burnt up at once, and the Princess knew that this man also had not fulfilled his word. So the Third Knight failed also.

Now the Fourth Knight was no more enterprising than the rest. Instead of starting out on the quest of the dragon bearing on its head the five-color-radiating jewel, he called all his servants together and gave them the order to seek for it far and wide in Japan and in China, and he strictly forbade any of them to return till they had found it.

His numerous retainers and servants started out in different directions, with no intention, however, of obeying what they considered an impossible order. They simply took a holiday, went to pleasant country places together, and grumbled at their master's unreasonableness.

The Knight meanwhile, thinking that his retainers could not fail to find the jewel, repaired to his house, and fitted it up beautifully for the reception of the Princess, he felt so sure of winning her. One year passed away in weary waiting, and still his men did not return with the dragon-jewel. The Knight became desperate. He could wait no longer, so taking with him only two men he hired a ship and commanded the captain to go in search of the dragon; the captain and the sailors refused to undertake what they said was an absurd search, but the Knight compelled them at last to put out to sea.

When they had been but a few days out they encountered a great storm which lasted so long that, by the time its fury abated, the Knight had determined to give up the hunt of the dragon. They were at last blown on shore, for navigation was primitive in those days. Worn out with his travels and anxiety, the fourth suitor gave himself up to rest. He had caught a very heavy cold, and had to go to bed with a swollen face.

The governor of the place, hearing of his plight, sent messengers with a letter inviting him to his house. While he was there thinking over all his troubles, his love for the Princess turned to anger, and he blamed her for all the hardships he had undergone. He thought that it was quite probable she had wished to kill him so that she might be rid of him, and in order to carry out her wish had sent him upon his impossible quest.

At this point all the servants he had sent out to find the jewel came to see him, and were surprised to find praise instead of displeasure awaiting them. Their master told them that he was heartily sick of adventure, and said that he never intended to go near the Princess's house again in the future. Like all the rest, the Fifth Knight failed in his quest--he could not find the swallow's shell. By this time the fame of Princess Moonlight's beauty had reached the ears of the Emperor, and he sent one of the Court ladies to see if she were really as lovely as report said; if so he would summon her to the Palace and make her one of the ladies-in-waiting.

When the Court lady arrived, in spite of her father's entreaties, Princess Moonlight refused to see her. The Imperial messenger insisted, saying it was the Emperor's order. Then Princess Moonlight told the old man that if she was forced to go to the Palace in obedience to the Emperor's order, she would vanish from the earth.

When the Emperor was told of her persistence in refusing to obey his summons, and that if pressed to obey she would disappear altogether from sight, he determined to go and see her. So he planned to go on a hunting excursion in the neighborhood of the bamboo-cutter's house, and see the Princess himself. He sent word to the old man of his intention, and he received consent to the scheme. The next day the Emperor set out with his retinue, which he soon managed to outride. He found the bamboo-cutter's house and dismounted. He then entered the house and went straight to where the Princess was sitting with her attendant maidens.

Never had he seen any one so wonderfully beautiful, and he could not but look at her, for she was more lovely than any human being as she shone in her own soft radiance. When Princess Moonlight became aware that a stranger was looking at her she tried to escape from the room, but the Emperor caught her and begged her to listen to what he had to say. Her only answer was to hide her face in her sleeves.

The Emperor fell deeply in love with her, and begged her to come to the Court, where he would give her a position of honor and everything she could wish for. He was about to send for one of the Imperial palanquins to take her back with him at once, saying that her grace and beauty should adorn a Court, and not be hidden in a bamboo-cutter's cottage.

But the Princess stopped him. She said that if she were forced to go to the Palace she would turn at once into a shadow, and even as she spoke she began to lose her form. Her figure faded from his sight while he looked.

The Emperor then promised to leave her free if only she would resume her former shape, which she did.

It was now time for him to return, for his retinue would be wondering what had happened to their Royal master when they missed him for so long. So he bade her good-by, and left the house with a sad heart. Princess Moonlight was for him the most beautiful woman in the world; all others were dark beside her, and he thought of her night and day. His Majesty now spent much of his time in writing poems, telling her of his love and devotion, and sent them to her, and though she refused to see him again she answered with many verses of her own composing, which told him gently and kindly that she could never marry any one on this earth. These little songs always gave him pleasure.

At this time her foster-parents noticed that night after night the Princess would sit on her balcony and gaze for hours at the moon, in a spirit of the deepest dejection, ending always in a burst of tears. One night the old man found her thus weeping as if her heart were broken, and he besought her to tell him the reason of her sorrow.

With many tears she told him that he had guessed rightly when he supposed her not to belong to this world--that she had in truth come from the moon, and that her time on earth would soon be over. On the fifteenth day of that very month of August her friends from the moon would come to fetch her, and she would have to return. Her parents were both there, but having spent a lifetime on the earth she had forgotten them, and also the moon-world to which she belonged. It made her weep, she said, to think of leaving her kind foster-parents, and the home where she had been happy for so long.

When her attendants heard this they were very sad, and could not eat or drink for sadness at the thought that the Princess was so soon to leave them.

The Emperor, as soon as the news was carried to him, sent messengers to the house to find out if the report were true or not.

The old bamboo-cutter went out to meet the Imperial messengers. The last few days of sorrow had told upon the old man; he had aged greatly, and looked much more than his seventy years. Weeping bitterly, he told them that the report was only too true, but he intended, however, to make prisoners of the envoys from the moon, and to do all he could to prevent the Princess from being carried back.

The men returned and told His Majesty all that had passed. On the fifteenth day of that month the Emperor sent a guard of two thousand warriors to watch the house. One thousand stationed themselves on the roof, another thousand kept watch round all the entrances of the house. All were well trained archers, with bows and arrows. The bamboo-cutter and his wife hid Princess Moonlight in an inner room.

The old man gave orders that no one was to sleep that night, all in the house were to keep a strict watch, and be ready to protect the Princess. With these precautions, and the help of the Emperor's men-at-arms, he hoped to withstand the moon-messengers, but the Princess told him that all these measures to keep her would be useless, and that when her people came for her nothing whatever could prevent them from carrying out their purpose. Even the Emperors men would be powerless. Then she added with tears that she was very, very sorry to leave him and his wife, whom she had learned to love as her parents, that if she could do as she liked she would stay with them in their old age, and try to make some return for all the love and kindness they had showered upon her during all her earthly life.

The night wore on! The yellow harvest moon rose high in the heavens, flooding the world asleep with her golden light. Silence reigned over the pine and the bamboo forests, and on the roof where the thousand men-at-arms waited.

Then the night grew gray towards the dawn and all hoped that the danger was over--that Princess Moonlight would not have to leave them after all. Then suddenly the watchers saw a cloud form round the moon--and while they looked this cloud began to roll earthwards. Nearer and nearer it came, and every one saw with dismay that its course lay towards the house.

In a short time the sky was entirely obscured, till at last the cloud lay over the dwelling only ten feet off the ground. In the midst of the cloud there stood a flying chariot, and in the chariot a band of luminous beings. One amongst them who looked like a king and appeared to be the chief stepped out of the chariot, and, poised in air, called to the old man to come out.

"The time has come," he said, "for Princess Moonlight to return to the moon from whence she came. She committed a grave fault, and as a punishment was sent to live down here for a time. We know what good care you have taken of the Princess, and we have rewarded you for this and have sent you wealth and prosperity. We put the gold in the bamboos for you to find."

"I have brought up this Princess for twenty years and never once has she done a wrong thing, therefore the lady you are seeking cannot be this one," said the old man. "I pray you to look elsewhere."

Then the messenger called aloud, saying:

"Princess Moonlight, come out from this lowly dwelling. Rest not here another moment."

At these words the screens of the Princess's room slid open of their own accord, revealing the Princess shining in her own radiance, bright and wonderful and full of beauty.

The messenger led her forth and placed her in the chariot. She looked back, and saw with pity the deep sorrow of the old man. She spoke to him many comforting words, and told him that it was not her will to leave him and that he must always think of her when looking at the moon.

The bamboo-cutter implored to be allowed to accompany her, but this was not allowed. The Princess took off her embroidered outer garment and gave it to him as a keepsake.

One of the moon beings in the chariot held a wonderful coat of wings, another had a phial full of the Elixir of Life which was given the Princess to drink. She swallowed a little and was about to give the rest to the old man, but she was prevented from doing so.

The robe of wings was about to be put upon her shoulders, but she said:

"Wait a little. I must not forget my good friend the Emperor. I must write him once more to say good-by while still in this human form."

In spite of the impatience of the messengers and charioteers she kept them waiting while she wrote. She placed the phial of the Elixir of Life with the letter, and, giving them to the old man, she asked him to deliver them to the Emperor.

Then the chariot began to roll heavenwards towards the moon, and as they all gazed with tearful eyes at the receding Princess, the dawn broke, and in the rosy light of day the moon-chariot and all in it were lost amongst the fleecy clouds that were now wafted across the sky on the wings of the morning wind.

Princess Moonlight's letter was carried to the Palace. His Majesty was afraid to touch the Elixir of Life, so he sent it with the letter to the top of the most sacred mountain in the land. Mount Fuji, and there the Royal emissaries burnt it on the summit at sunrise. So to this day people say there is smoke to be seen rising from the top of Mount Fuji to the clouds.

27

Printed in Great Britain
by Amazon